PETRO
The Brave Little Cargo Plane

Written and illustrated by

P.C. Kell

Pretty Cool Books
St. Louis, MO

For Bethany, Shannon
and Mariah

The Gift
Life has its ups and downs
Filled with blessings and disasters
Yet no matter how low we're bound
Hope is always there to grasp for

Petro, The Brave Little Cargo Plane
Written and illustrated by P.C. Kell

ISBN: 978-1-7328341-0-8

Printed in the United States of America

Published by Pretty Cool Books, St. Louis, Missouri
3725 Courtois Street, St. Louis, MO 63123
PrettyCoolBooks.com pckellbooks@gmail.com

CHAPTER 1

Wingin' It

Petro sat in front of an old barn as the morning sun rose above the farm fields. The shiny new airplane felt the warm beams of light along his bright yellow wings and smiled. This was the day he was going to fly for the first time! All was quiet— until he heard a voice calling from a tall oak tree.

"Hi there," said a curious young sparrow. "What kind of a bird are you?"
Petro looked at the sparrow and wondered about that himself.

From a higher branch, a robin chuckled. "That's not a bird you're speaking
to brother sparrow. That's an airplane."

"From here he looks like a big yellow canary," said a mockingbird as she
fed her young.

"Confound that contraption!" growled a sleepy owl. "I don't like it. Not one bit."

"What's bothering you so much?" asked the robin.

4

"That flyin' machine was built with scrap metal from the old grain silo," said the owl. "That place, well…it's haunted!"

"Don't be silly," said the robin. "That silo was wrecked years ago by a falling star. There's nothing haunted about that."

"You're wrong," said the owl. "I saw a strange and eerie glow there one night last winter. Like that star had come to life again!"

Just then, a howling wind blew across the meadow, followed by the sound of a creaking door.

Coming out of the barn, it was Farmer McDoon and his grandson Maxie. They had spent weeks building the little airplane and were now getting him ready to fly.

"Let's roll him out and get started," said Grandfather.

"Sure thing," Maxie replied.

When they reached a field of tall grass, Maxie climbed into Petro's cockpit and turned the switch to start the motor. "When I yell 'contact'," said Maxie, "give the propeller a good crank."

Petro's nose tickled as Grandfather took hold of his propeller. When Maxie gave the signal, the old farmer gave it a crank to get the motor going.

"PET-RO...PET...RO....PET....RO," the motor sputtered as the propeller spun to a stop.

"Let's try again," said Grandfather.

Once more, Maxie shouted, "Contact!"

This time, Grandfather cranked with all his might.

"PET-RO-PET-RO-PET-RO-PET-RO," the motor puttered and shuddered.

Suddenly, Petro's propeller was spinning faster and faster until his motor let out a loud and powerful "PETROOOOOOOM!"

Petro rattled and shook with delight as his motor roared. Then Maxie drove the plane forward to begin the flight.

Picking up speed, Petro scurried through the field as the birds flew along.

"Look at him go!" cheered the sparrow.

"Noisy contraption!" squawked the owl. "That boy has no business flying that thing."

"But Maxie's had plenty of flying lessons," said the robin.

"Well, he'd better start using them," warned the owl, "because it looks like he's headed for a crash.

Sure enough, the cranky old owl was right. Petro was gaining speed but struggling to get off the ground.

"Oh no!" cried the sparrow. "He's heading straight into the chicken coops!"

"He'll never clear them in time," said the robin.

"Tsk,tsk," quipped the owl. "Not enough power to fly, I suppose."

At that moment, Petro's metal panels gave off a bright and mysterious glow as a fiery streak of light came rushing out of his wings and tail. Then, with his motor roaring "PET-ROOOOOOOM!" he swooped up, missing the chicken coops by inches!

"What on earth just happened?" asked the robin.

"Some…some…something not of this earth," stuttered the startled owl.

Like a shooting star, Petro flew high in the sky as Maxie guided him toward the windswept clouds. It wasn't long before the entire countryside was in view. Houses and barns had shrunk to the size of matchboxes, while people and farm animals looked no bigger than insects. All looked peaceful, until they saw a group of crows invading Grandfather's cornpatch.

The notorious band was led by Mortimer, meanest crow in the county. Donning a corncob crown, the bird brought his flock into the patch each summer to destroy everything in sight.

Grandfather had tried chasing them away, but nothing worked. If one crow flew out, another would fly over from behind. Worst of all, the wicked birds laughed while playing their evil game.

"Let's teach those crows a lesson," shouted Maxie.

Petro's motor revved in agreement.

Right away, Maxie and Petro turned and raced for the cornpatch. At top speed, they swooped over the crows like divebombers.

"PET-ROOOOOOOM!" Petro roared.

In a heartbeat, the crows scattered like frightened rabbits, leaving the patch and their tail feathers far behind.

Grandfather smiled and waved thanks to Maxie and Petro for the rescue, and the two flew off into the western sky.

CHAPTER 2
The Fire Flies!

Gliding high over miles of farm fields, Maxie and Petro soon reached a small country town. On its outskirts was a fairground where grandstands filled with people towered over a runway crowded with rumbling airplanes.

Petro flew over the spectacle thinking he was just passing through, but Maxie had something else in mind.

"There it is!" the boy shouted. "The starting line to the Crawdad County air race. I just know we're going to win!"

Petro's motor burst a happy hum. An air race sounded like fun! But soon after they landed, the little airplane became troubled.

All around him were bigger planes with large and powerful motors.

"How can I compete in a race against them?" Petro wondered. To make matters worse, some of the pilots started to point at him and snicker.

"Kind of puny, isn't he?" said one.

"Nothin' more than a puddle jumper," scoffed another.

Petro's hopes of winning the race were sinking fast.

"Pay no mind to them," reassured Maxie. "You may be small but you're lightening fast! Why, we can outfly any airplane here. Just wait and see!"

With that said, Petro's spirits soared. Boldly revving his motor, he was ready to beat them all to the finish.

Moments later, the pilots brought their planes to the starting line.

"Four times around the water tower and back," announced the judge. "The first one to reach the finish line wins the grand prize, a brand new Filberton farm tractor. Good luck!"

"That's just what Grandfather needs for the farm," said Maxie as he waited for the signal to start.

Petro's motor was in full roar when the flag was dropped and they bolted down the runway. One by one, the planes took to the air, flying as fast as they could, rounding the water tower and heading back to the main grandstand.

Petro led them all in the first lap, but in the second, he fell behind. By the end of the third he was running last.

Maxie's hopes of winning the race were fading as the other planes passed them by. Still detemined, he tried to catch up.

"Tough luck, kid," one of the other pilots bellowed.

"Come back when you grow up," cracked another.

"Leave the racing to the real pilots," howled one more.

The insults brought Petro's motor oil to a boil! The pilots could mock *him* all they wanted, but not Maxie. That was going too far!

In a flash, Petro's metal panels lit the sky with a blinding glow. With his motor heaving a powerful roar, he shot forward like a blazing rocket, zipping past every airplane ahead and leaving their pilots quivering in disbelief.

"Jumpin' fireflies!" cried Maxie. "We're in the lead again!"

Heading into the last turn, the race was theirs to win...until something terrible happened.

A small boy watching the race on the water tower fell from the railing. He was caught by an older boy, but was dangling in the path of the speeding airplane. Maxie quickly steered away from the structure, causing Petro's rudder to break. Suddenly, the little plane lost control. Swaying wildly back and forth, Petro flew out of the fairgrounds, down a hill, and into a tree-covered valley.

"Oh, no!" cried Maxie. "We're losing altitude!"

As each second passed, Petro was coming closer to a crash. Searching ahead, Maxie found a clearing safe enough to land in. If they could just get over a few trees, they would be out of danger. Then, something brushed against the airplane's landing gear.

CHAPTER 3

A Flight Of Misfortunes

A high branch snagged one of Petro's tires, causing a blowout. Landing with the damage led to a terrible jolt, sending the plane scrambling out of control.

Maxie held on tight as Petro cut through a wheat field, broke through a wood fence, plowed into a pigpen, broke through another fence, ripped down a clothesline, then headed for a farmhouse!

Petro came to a sudden stop just inches away from the building.

"Whew," Maxie sighed. "That was a close one."

As the boy climbed out of the plane's cockpit, however, he was startled by an angry voice.

"What in tarnation is going on here?" a burly man shouted as he stormed out of his farmhouse.

At that moment, Maxie realized he had landed Petro right in the middle of Wiley Fogbaum's farm. And Wiley was furious!

"Just look what your plane did to my wheatfield and pigpen!" he growled. "Not to mention my best pairs of long johns!"

"Well, you see Mr. Fogbaum," Maxie explained. "We were in this race and…"

"Never mind excuses," Wiley interrupted. "How do you intend to pay for all this damage?"

Maxie trembled as he searched through his empty pockets, trying to think of a way to pay for the wreckage.

Petro was getting worried as well. Covered in mud and long johns, the little plane shook as Wiley gave him a sinister glare.

"Tell you what, son," said Wiley. "I know a thing or two about these flyin' machines. I'll call it even if you let me have yours. Otherwise your grandfather will have to pay for this mess."

Maxie hated the thought of giving up the airplane he cherished so much, but he felt he had no other choice.

"All right," the boy muttered. "The airplane is yours."

"Great!" shouted Wiley, "And don't worry kid, I'll take good care of him."

Petro could only hope that Wiley would keep his word. As he watched Maxie sadly walk away for the last time, the little plane sat heartbroken and troubled over what was ahead.

The next morning Wiley chained a tractor to Petro and pulled him into a pasture.

"I'll have you ready to fly in no time," said Wiley as he started repairing the plane's landing gear and tail.

When Wiley installed an odd-looking container and connected it to pipes running under Petro's cockpit and wings, the little plane was puzzled.

"That does it," said Wiley as he turned the last screw. "Now we're ready to dust some lima beans.

"So that's it!" Petro realized. "I've been turned into a crop-dusting plane."

Wiley filled the container with a bag of bug-killer and flew over to his bean field. He lowered the plane close to the ground and pulled a lever that released the poisonous powder.

"This'll kill them pesky bugs!" Wiley bellowed.

As the powder streamed out of Petro's wings, a cloud of thick, toxic dust rose from the ground, choking his motor.

"Pet-choo! Pet-choo!" Petro sneezed as his motor gasped for air. "Pet-chunk! Pet-chunk!" he coughed as his power grew weaker and weaker.

"Come on, get going, you no- good bucket of bolts!" yelled Wiley.

It was no use. Petro was suffocating from the deadly dust. If he didn't leave the bean field soon his motor would sputter to a stop.

With a growl, Wiley turned the airplane around and headed back. After they landed, the farmer leaped out of the cockpit and stormed off to a nearby shed.

"Uh, oh," Petro shuttered. "I'm in real trouble now."

A moment later, Wiley returned swinging a large hammer.

"You worthless pile of junk!" he shouted. "No machine ever acts up on me that way!"

As Petro braced himself to be bashed to bits, Wiley took the hammer over to a fence post instead. He nailed a sign to it that said AIRPLANE FOR SALE, then rushed off to do other chores.

Relieved to still be in one piece, Petro let out a restful sigh. Wiley was through with him.

And thank goodness he was out of the crop-dusting business! But after the little airplane sat alone and idle for months he wondered if he would ever be sold.

Then one day a man from the Army Air Corps came by looking for an airplane to help him train his new recruits.

"He's smaller than the planes we normally use," said the officer as he gave Petro a close inspection.

"If you take him now, I'll sell for half the price," said Wiley.

The officer agreed to the deal and the next day Petro was back in the air, happy to be flying again. When the little plane arrived at his new home, however, his happiness soon turned to disappointment.

CHAPTER 4

Crushers and Clowns

After landing on an airfield, Petro was taken to a hangar for a new coat of paint. Then he was rushed to the runway of a flight school to be used as a trainer for new pilots.

In the days that followed, Petro was flown by the raw recruits, going through repeated rough-and-tumble landings that sent him to the repair shop almost every night.

Late one evening as Petro's tire was getting patched, the decision was made that the Air Corps no longer needed him. After months of abuse, his motor was worn to a frazzle and his metal panels were coming apart at the seams. But instead of getting repaired, he was being sent to the army surplus yard…to be turned into scrap!

The next morning Petro was towed to a scrapyard where he found himself surrounded by broken-down tanks, ragged jeeps and rusted out supply trucks. The place was peaceful for a time, until a monsterous machine sitting across the yard got to work.

With vultures perched over its huge frame, the smoke billowing mammouth made a screeching "Ker-plunkity-plunk-plunk-plunk" noise as it crushed big hunks of metal down to the size of soup cans!

Petro rattled with terror as workmen moved him closer each hour toward the dreaded machine. Just before the plane was set to be shoved into the contraption's deadly jaws, a man in colorful suit showed up.

"Say, I kind of like this one," he said. "He'll be perfect for my new show."

"He's yours for twenty bucks if you get him off the lot before sunset," replied the yardmaster

Petro heaved a sigh of relief when the man handed over the money. The plane was then hooked to the back of the man's truck and hauled away.

When they reached an empty flight field, the man backed Petro into a hangar, where a crew of mechanics got busy making repairs. Within a few days, Petro's motor was rebuilt and running smooth. His holes were patched and dents were straightened. Petro was feeling like a new plane again, but noticed something different.

Painted purple with pink polka dots, Petro was now the newest member of Claude Crump's Flying Circus and Daredevil Act! Joining three other airplanes, he became part of an aerial performance troop that barnstormed across the great Midwest.

Flown by a pilot dressed as a clown, Petro did silly maneuvers in an amusing sideshow that brought laughter to every audience. The entertainment became serious, though, when the other airplanes took over.

After landing far away from the fairgrounds, Petro watched in envy as the others performed death-defying stunts. The crowds roared with excitement as they flew upside down, raced through fire, and looped around one another.

"I could do those stunts if they'd let me," Petro thought to himself.

Then, one dark evening, the little plane was awakened by the sound of cackling voices.

CHAPTER 5

The Big Stunt

Perched on the door to Petro's shed were three crows staring down at him. "See Morty," one them said, "I told you he was purple with pink polka dots."

"Sorry, Milton," said Mortimer. "I thought you were seeing things again."

"Aw, Morty," said Milton. "Just because I thought that farmer was a scarecrow."

"And you almost got us shot!" the third one scolded.

"Never mind that, T-Bone," said Mortimer. "An airplane can't be taken seriously with colors like those."

"That's right," T-Bone agreed. "What this guy needs is a stunt."

"Yeah," Milton added. "A special stunt."

As Mortimer scratched his beak, an idea came to him. "The Triple Axle Loop-De-Loop ought to do the trick," he suggested.

"A Triple what?" asked Milton.

"You know," Mortimer explained. "It's the stunt where you turn upside down. Then you, er… what comes next, T-Bone?"

"Oh yeah," said T-Bone. Then you, um… loop three times around. What comes next, Milty?"

Milton ruffled his brow. "Oh, I know!" he chortled. "You dive straight to the ground!"

Petro had never heard of such a stunt. It sounded far too dangerous and he wondered if the birds were up to something sneaky.

While thinking it over, Petro noticed Mortimer's corncob crown and remembered him and his companions. They were the same crows he and Maxie chased out of Grandfather's corn patch!

A moment later, Petro felt something odd. Milton and T-Bone were loosening the cables that controlled his wing flaps.

"Just a few more adjustments," T-Bone smirked, "and you'll be ready for your big stunt."

"It'll be a cinch," Milton giggled.

"And don't forget," Mortimer snickered, "we'll be watching."

After the crows left, Petro became worried about the next day's flight. But when the show started, his performance seemed better than ever. The crowds that once laughed were now cheering as he flew upside down, looped around, and raced high in the sky. All went well- until there was a loud and sudden snap. Petro's wing controls broke loose and the pilot parachuted out. The airplane was heading for a crash!

Petro spiraled to earth, then smashed through the roof of a deserted barn. When he hit the ground, his fuel line broke and a tremendous fire erupted. Firefighters rushed to put out the blaze, but it was too late. The fiery crash left the plane charred and mangled beyond repair.

Hours after the smoke cleared, Petro woke up dazed and confused. When he saw his reflection in a pool of water, he gasped in horror.

"What happened?" Petro wondered.

"Looks like you fell down and went boom," someone said with a giggle.

Petro looked up and saw Mortimer, Milton and T-Bone roosting in the burned-out hayloft.

"Nice try pal," said Mortimer. "You were just a little short on that last loop."

"That was one wild dive, man," said T-Bone.

"Yeah," Milton agreed. "Even better than the one you showed us in Farmer McDoon's corn patch."

Petro gave the crows an angry glare.

"If I could get those mangy buzzards within an inch of my propeller," he fumed, "I'd show them a thing or two!"

But when Petro viewed his twisted propeller and fractured wings, he knew their devious trick had left him permanently grounded. Mulling over the terrible situation, the plane heard a disturbing growl.

It was coming from T-Bone's stomach. "Hey guys," said the crow, "Old Faithful's telling me it's time for dinner."

"I hear the Bixbys are growing a lovely cuisine this season," said Milton in mock elegance.

"Well, one thing's for sure," Mortimer snickered. "we won't have to worry about our meals being interrupted by this chump anymore. Let's go!"

After the crows flew away, Petro let out a long, sad sigh. Having failed at everything from dusting crops to air racing, he was now nothing but a defeated wreck; a plane that had reached rock bottom.

Petro knew it would be a miracle if he were ever to fly again. But what he didn't know was that miraculous things can happen when you reach the bottom, because you have nowhere else to go…but up!

Alone and abandoned, Petro remained in the burned out barn for many years. With no one to care for him, his wooden frame began to rot. Countless rainstorms turned his metal panels to rust. But worst of all, his spirits fell into deep despair. Everything seemed hopeless for the little plane...until darkness came one cold Christmas Eve.

As midnight approached, a terrible blizzard arrived in the valley, bringing heavy sleet and blinding snow. Petro shivered as an icy blanket of white covered him, piling higher with each passing minute.

"Being buried in snow will be the final blow," he thought.

Then something wonderful happened.

The snow stopped falling. Then the wind turned calm and the clouds rushed away. Off in the distance, a gleaming light appeared in the heavens.

Petro gazed up and saw a wonderous star, bigger and brighter than any he'd ever seen, shining over him. As its warmth melted away the ice and snow, the little plane felt his spirits lifting again. No longer in despair, his rusty metal panels began to glow for the first time in years.

For Petro, the yuletide star not only gave him back his hope, but lit a path that would reunite him with an old friend.

CHAPTER 6

The Homecoming

Not long after the stars arrival, Petro saw an old truck trudging through the snow. As it headed up the road, the little plane worried that its driver might be a junkman searching for scrap.

When the truck stopped nearby, a grey-haired man stepped out. Listening to his footsteps crunch through the snow, the plane began to tremble.

"Maybe he won't find me in the shadows." Petro hoped.

But when the old man crept into the barn, he discovered Petro's faint glow looming in the darkness. Beaming his flashlight toward the mysterious sight, he was overcome with joy when he found the mangled airplane.

"Jumpin' fireflies!" the man shouted. "If you aren't a sight for sore eyes! "

Petro was bewildered by the old timer's commotion. " Why is this fellow so excited over finding a broken-down airplane?" he wondered.

As the man came closer, Petro noticed something familiar. Behind the wrinkles, eyeglasses, and fuzzy white mustache, the eyes and face reminded him of someone. Then the plane felt the old man touching his battered nose and knew. It was Maxie!

"Lucky I was driving my tow truck tonight," said Maxie. "Why, I'll have you out of here in no time."

Petro's rusty frown squeaked into a cheerful smile. Rescued at last, he was finally going home. But as Maxie hauled him away from the barn, a sudden gust of wind caused the decaying structure to come crashing down with a mighty BOOM!

"Whew," Maxie sighed. "It's a miracle we got out in time."

Petro knew it was a miracle, too. Traveling in tow down the snowy road, the little plane looked up once more at the star that saved him and smiled. But as he watched the star twinkle, little did he know that one day he would be called on to perform a miracle of his own, a great task that would take all his courage.

Through the winter months, Maxie worked on Petro in his warm garage. Piece by piece, he carefully restored the plane until it was looking like new again. By late spring, the old pilot finished the job by installing a small cargo door behind the cockpit.

"Now we can carry supplies with us on long trips," said Maxie, "since our racing days are over."

The next morning he rolled Petro out to his pasture to start the motor.

"PET…RO…PET…RO…PET-RO…PET-RO…PET-ROOOOOM!" the plane roared.

Petro was thrilled to hear his motor running again…and amazed that it started on the first try!

Soaring up into the sky, the two were soon flying high enough to see the entire countryside. Everything was pleasant and peaceful, until something disturbing appeared below.

A band of crows were devouring Maxie's corn patch. Petro took one look at the corncob crown and knew it was Mortimer and his gang.

As the birds filled their bellies, Mortimer looked up in the sky and turned pale with fear when he saw the airplane.

"It can't be!" he shrieked. "It must be a ghost!"

"You're beginning to look like one," said T-Bone.

"Yeah," Milton agreed. "What's the big deal, boss?"

When Mortimer pointed up, the birds gawked in disbelief.

"Let's show those crows what a couple of old timers can do!" yelled Maxie.

Petro reared back his nose like a charging bull and he and Maxie swooped over the crows like a dive-bomber.

"PET-ROOOOOOOOOOOOM!" Petro roared.

Crow feathers flew everywhere, and within seconds the terrified buzzards fled the valley for good.

"Yahoo!" Maxie cheered. "We showed those crows a thing or two, didn't we?"

Petro's motor hummed in happy agreement.

Flying up again, peace returned to the valley, but dark clouds were gathering on the horizon.

"We better start back," warned Maxie. "It looks like a powerful storm is headed our way."

But before he could turn Petro around, a bright red flare burst into the sky.

"That's a distress signal," cried Maxie. "Someone's in trouble!"

CHAPTER 7

The Daring Rescue

A few miles away they found a large cargo jet stranded in a field of mud. Landing Petro nearby, Maxie dashed over to see if the pilots needed their help. As he spoke to the men, the little plane heard how they were forced down by a terrible storm and that they were carrying emergency supplies which needed to get to a flooded town.

"It's a matter of life or death!" the pilots declared.

Petro gazed at the huge jet towering over him and wondered what his chances were of getting through the storm.

"I have to do it," he decided. "Lives are depending on me."

After two small crates of rescue supplies were loaded into Petro's cargo hold, Maxie and Petro began their perilous mission, flying into a dark and turbulent sky.

As they traveled east, the air turned cold. Fierce winds tossed them about while heavy rain came pouring down like a waterfall.

Then, a dark and monstrous thundercloud appeared, turning the sky pitch black as it shot thunder and lightening out of its belly like cannon fire.

Maxie and Petro fought past every danger, but when they reached the storm cloud, a powerful headwind blew them back. Desperately trying to break through, a lightning bolt struck Petro's rudder. Suddenly, the little plane was sent into a tailspin.

"Oh, no!" cried Maxie. "We're done for!"

As they plummeted to earth, all seemed lost. Then Petro remembered his special gift. It was a power greater than anything on earth!

At that moment, the little plane broke free from his fall and soared into a valley. Circling over a field, his metal panels began to glow brighter than ever. A shower of sparks shot out of his wings and tail, bathing the valley with an incredible rainbow of fiery colors.

Seconds later, the plane raced up into the sky and headed toward the evil cloud, blasting into its billows with a loud and terrible…

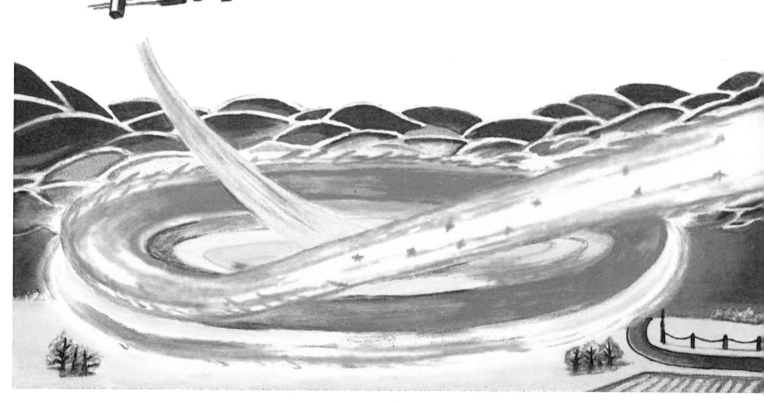

The tremendous explosion broke the storm and shook the heavens. Then, as the sky turned blue again, Maxie and Petro came roaring out of the clouds like a flaming meteor!

Surviving the encounter with only a scratch, they were now within a few miles of the flooded town.

When the two arrived, they discovered a rising river and children stranded on the roof of a schoolhouse surrounded by water. Petro landed in a clearing nearby and the townspeople rushed over in a panic.

"Thank goodness you're here," one woman cried. "Our children are in grave danger."

But when Maxie unloaded Petro's cargo, the residents were disappointed. There were just two little crates, one long and the other short, not enough supply needed for the rescue, many thought. As the boxes were opened, though, everyone was pleasantly surprised.

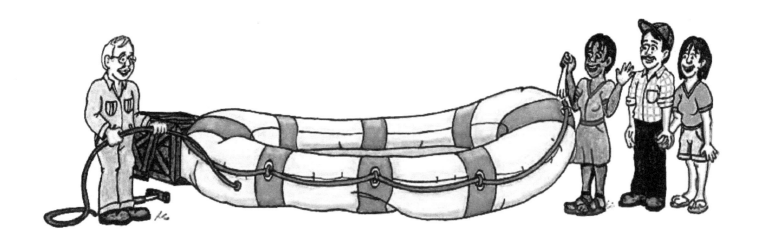

Reaching into the short box, Maxie pulled out a cord that inflated a huge life raft.

"Here are the oars!" shouted a man that opened the long box. "Let's get our kids off that roof!"

Within minutes, all the children and their teachers were rescued. Late that afternoon the floodwaters were receding and Maxie was celebrated as the town's brave new hero, but all the time he knew who had really saved the day…

That evening Petro looked up to the stars. As he watched them twinkle, he thought of all the terrible things he'd gone through to get to where he was and never felt more content. He wasn't a race plane, crop-duster, flight trainer, or barnstorming sideshow act. He was a storm-busting cargo plane! And what on earth could be better than that?

The Petro Flying Machine
Pretty Cool Aeronautics, Inc., USA

Designed and constructed by Maxie McDoon and his Grandfather, this airplane is powered by a six-cylinder Braggs & Sternly engine.
Metal panels for the body and wings were salvaged from an old grain silo struck by a falling star. Top engine speed: 116 mph.
Top speed of activated metal panels: 156, 412 mph. Petro is an airplane well-suited for stormbusting and high-priority rescue missions.

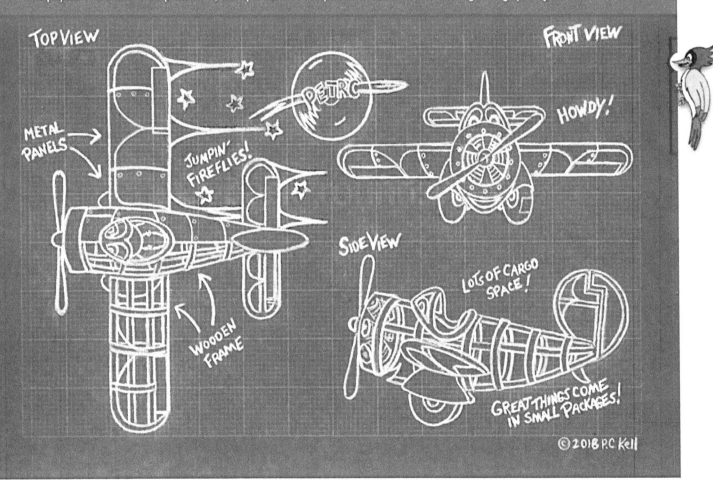

TOP VIEW

FRONT VIEW

PETRO

HOWDY!

METAL PANELS

JUMPIN' FIREFLIES!

WOODEN FRAME

SIDE VIEW

LOTS OF CARGO SPACE!

GREAT THINGS COME IN SMALL PACKAGES!

© 2018 P.C. Kell

75

Thank you for reading **Petro, the Brave Little Cargo Plane**. I hope you found it enjoyable. Your feedback is important to me. Please take a few minutes to write a brief review on Amazon.

...And drop me a line at pckellbooks@gmail.com. I would enjoy hearing from you!

-P.C. Kell

P.C. Kell, a former first responder and illustrator for *Young Equestrian* magazine, grew up in a home where one of the greatest joys were the times when he and his family watched cartoons and animated films together. Working as a freelance artist for various youth-based magazines and periodicals over the years, P.C. has always dreamed of creating that same kind of joy for children by writing and illustrating memorable stories that will entertain and teach positive values.

9 781732 834118